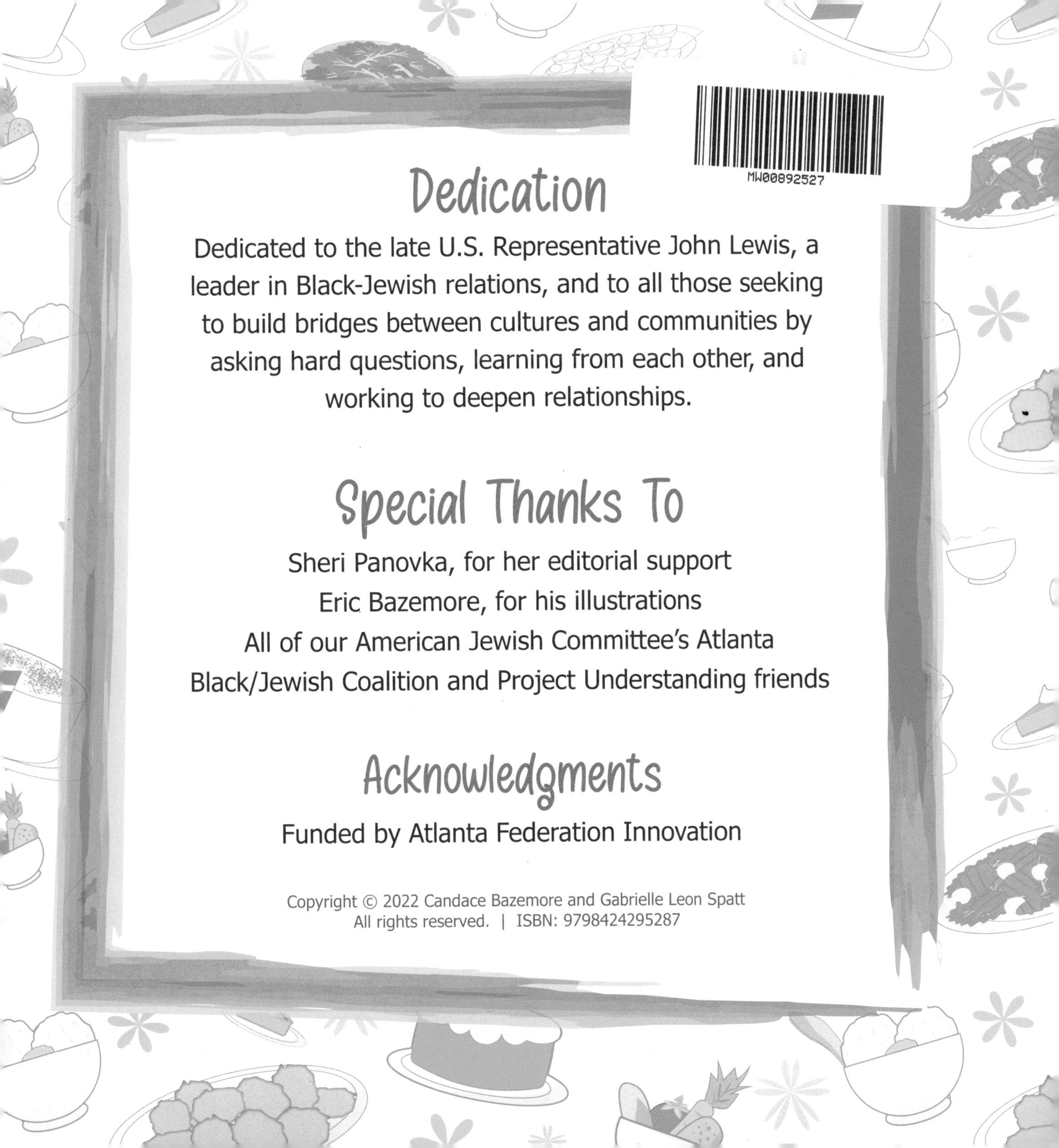

Dedication

Dedicated to the late U.S. Representative John Lewis, a leader in Black-Jewish relations, and to all those seeking to build bridges between cultures and communities by asking hard questions, learning from each other, and working to deepen relationships.

Special Thanks To

Sheri Panovka, for her editorial support
Eric Bazemore, for his illustrations
All of our American Jewish Committee's Atlanta Black/Jewish Coalition and Project Understanding friends

Acknowledgments

Funded by Atlanta Federation Innovation

 | ISBN: 9798424295287

David and Malcolm have been best friends since kindergarten. They are now in Mr. Torres' third grade class.

Mr. Torres has traveled the world and loves to share stories and experiences from different places he has visited. He especially likes to talk about the people he meets and the things he learns from them.

The next topic in Mr. Torres' class is going to be family traditions. Mr. Torres asks his students to form groups of two and pick a family tradition to present.

Malcolm and David team up and eagerly volunteer to share their family dinner traditions.

David is really excited to talk about the Shabbat dinners he has every Friday with his family. Malcolm can't wait to describe his family's Sunday dinners and his favorite dishes.

Mr. Torres assigns them next Friday to present.

The boys talk about their presentations that day at lunch and during the entire ride home after school with Malcolm's mom.

Malcolm’s mom calls David’s mom to tell her about the boys’ nonstop excitement. The moms talk about the boys’ energy and about how wonderful it is that Mr. Torres believes so much in learning about other cultures and sharing their ritual experiences.

Over the next week, Malcolm and David work on their presentations with their parents' help.
They collect the items used at the dinners and talk about the special foods served and traditions they want to share with the class.

When Friday arrives, the boys are ready for their presentation. They both have prepared their notes and are eager to share with their friends.

To surprise David and Malcolm, Mr. Torres has invited their parents to attend the presentations.

"Shabbat shalom, y'all!"

David starts off his presentation with a loud "Shabbat shalom, y'all!"

Shabbat is Hebrew for "Sabbath," and "Shabbat shalom" means "Sabbath peace." It is a traditional greeting to welcome the holiday and share good wishes from sundown on Friday to sundown on Saturday.

David and Malcolm live in the South, where the word "y'all" is the way to say "you all."

David shows the class the table he has set with candles; a "kiddush" cup for wine or grape juice; challah, a traditional braided bread eaten on holidays; and a "siddur," the Jewish prayer book used for Shabbat and other holidays.

He explains the rituals that take place every Friday at sundown.

David turns the lights out in the classroom to pretend it's sunset, the official time when Jewish families light two candles to welcome Shabbat. He passes out a special card his mother has created so his classmates can join him in reciting the Shabbat blessing over the candles.

Mr. Torres helps light the candles, and David leads the class in the ancient Shabbat ritual prayer.

David tells his classmates the blessing over the candles is the first of several Shabbat prayers Jewish people across the globe recite every week.

David picks up the kiddush cup used to drink wine (or grape juice) on Shabbat. "This cup was given to my great-grandfather for his bar mitzvah, which is when someone reads from the Torah for the first time," he explains. "It has been passed down through multiple generations and lives at my grandpa's house now. He loaned it to me for today."

David leads the class in the blessing over the cup of wine/grape juice.

Then Malcolm asks David, "What smells so delicious?" David tells everyone it comes from the challah his mom baked early that morning. Challah is his favorite bread, and as he passes it out to his classmates, he explains how she braids and bakes it every week.

When everyone has a piece, David leads the blessing over the challah.

After reciting all the blessings, David's family enjoys a traditional meal with challah, matzo ball soup, a roasted chicken with potatoes and vegetables, and dessert. Other families might celebrate Shabbat differently, depending on their traditions, their cultures, and where they live.

Jewish communities can be found on every continent, and David explains how Jewish people around the world and even in the United States come in all shapes, sizes, and skin colors.

David has so much fun sharing his Shabbat traditions with everyone that he invites the entire class to come for dinner one Friday night.

His parents smile from the back of the room and say, "Yes! All are welcome!"

When David finishes, it's Malcolm's turn to talk about his family's Sunday dinners. Malcolm says hello and starts speaking.

"Once a month, my entire family gets together for dinner. We have a big gathering with lots of different dishes, and it's so much fun!"

Each Sunday dinner is different, depending on who hosts and who can come. Everyone is invited. "It's always a fun mix of my aunts, uncles, cousins, and, of course, my awesome grandparents!"

"When we have it at our house, my mom spends the entire day making a big home-cooked meal. Everyone loves to participate, so others bring the best parts...the side dishes and desserts!"

Each guest brings something special they like to make—collard greens, deviled eggs, mashed potatoes, rice and gravy, sweet potato pie, red velvet cake, and more.

"My favorites are red velvet cake and my mom's deep-fried cornbread," he says. "My mom even made a special batch of cornbread for everyone in the class to try."

"When the food is ready to be served, we all gather around the tables and bow our heads as the host says a prayer over the meal. Then we all say 'Amen!'

And then we eat!"

"My mom and my aunties help make plates for my grandparents.
Then everyone else makes their own plates.

During each dinner, we have great conversations as the entire family catches up on what's happened since our last Sunday dinner."

After the meal, when everyone has finished eating and they are cleaning up, the family usually has a group activity planned. The adults play cards, while the kids play board games or have a dance-off to music.

David and Malcolm's parents enjoy learning about Shabbat and Sunday dinners and invite each other over for dinner the following month.

David and Malcolm were surprised to learn how similar their family dinners and traditions are even with their different backgrounds. The boys can't wait to go to each other's homes for Shabbat and Sunday dinners. They are excited to meet each other's extended family, try the foods the other talked about, and experience each other's dinner traditions.

Continuing the conversation

The dinner table is a special place that can bring people, ideas, and cultures together. Use these conversation prompts for a future dinner with your family. Or invite another family over to join yours in conversation!

1. What is your favorite family tradition?

2. What is your favorite family dish to share with others?

3. What is your favorite memory about your family?

4. How do you keep your family traditions alive?

5. Who do you look up to as a role model and why?

6. Have you had a conversation with someone who thinks differently than you this week? If so, what did you learn?

About Black-Jewish Relations

Blacks and Jews have been connected throughout much of the history of the United States. One of the most important stories involves the Jewish community's support for the Black community during the Civil Rights Movement in the 1950s and 1960s. But even before then, Jewish-owned businesses were often friendly to Black customers. Rabbis, Jewish spiritual leaders, and other community leaders could often be seen walking hand in hand with Black leaders as they demonstrated for equal rights. Many referred to this as "praying with their feet."

Today, the two communities remain close and supportive of equal rights for all.

Rabbi Abraham Heschel with Dr. Martin Luther King, Jr. protesting at the beginning of the civil rights movement. Photo: Haarets.co.il

Challah recipe

(Makes two challahs)

Ingredients

2¼ tsp yeast • 1 tsp sugar • 1 cup of very warm water (almost too warm, but not too hot!)
2 eggs • 2 tsp salt • ¼ cup sugar • ⅓ cup oil • 4+ cups flour • one egg yolk for baking

Directions

Mix the yeast, sugar, and warm water together in a small bowl.
Let the mixture stand for approximately 10 minutes. The mixture will start to bubble.
Meanwhile, in a large mixing bowl, mix the 2 eggs, salt, sugar, oil, and 2 cups of flour together.
Add the yeast mixture to the flour mixture.
Add about 1½ cups of flour to the mixture. Start to form a ball of dough. As it comes together, it will separate from the bowl.
Place the dough on a floured surface, and punch it down to form a disc.
To knead it, lift up one side, fold it over, punch it down to form a disc again, and repeat it with each side. Knead it for at least 5 minutes as dough becomes increasingly elastic. If the dough is still sticky, add a bit more flour to it. Form the dough into a ball.
Place 2 tbsp of oil into a bowl and rub it around to coat the bottom and sides. Then place the dough into the oiled bowl, cover it, and place it somewhere warm for 1 – 1½ hours to rise,
until it's approximately double in size.
Preheat the oven to 375º. Remove the cover from the bowl, and place the dough on a floured surface.
Punch the dough out one more time and cut it in half, one for each challah. Then divide each half into 3 equal pieces. Roll out each piece, crimp together at the top, and braid the pieces into a loaf.
Place the loaf on a greased cookie sheet (you may use parchment paper or a silicone baking mat).
Repeat with the second ball of dough. You may let it rise again at this step.
Brush each challah with a mixture made with egg yolk and a few drops water.
Bake for about 25 – 30 minutes or until the bread rises and looks golden brown.
Remove oaves and place the on a cooling rack.
Place the challah on a platter, cover it, and wait for Shabbat dinner. Eat and enjoy!

This recipe is adapted from one shared by Beth Ricanati in her book Braided: A Journey of a Thousand Challahs.

Deep-Fried Cornbread recipe

(Makes 5 to 6 Servings)

Ingredients

1 cup self-rising cornmeal mix • 2/3 cup water • 1 cup vegetable oil (for frying)

Directions

Mix the first two ingredients to make a batter, adding more or less water depending on how thick or thin you want your cornbread patties.

In a skillet or frying pan, heat all the oil until it reaches medium heat, and test a small drop (½ a teaspoon) of batter. **You do not want to fry it too fast.**

Drop full tablespoons of batter in the oil, and pat them out with the back of a spoon to make a pattie.

Turn it over when the bottom is light brown

This recipe is similar to Candace's grandmother's.
Recipe source: food.com/recipe/fried-cornbread-southern-style-307995.

Meet the Authors

Gabby Leon Spatt and Candace Bazemore met while volunteering through the Junior League of Atlanta, a women's organization that promotes volunteerism, develops leaders, and inspires its members to effect positive change in the broader community. Their friendship solidified when they realized they both were also involved with the Atlanta Black/Jewish Coalition, an initiative of the American Jewish Committee (AJC) and co-founded by the late Congressman John Lewis. Their desire to learn from, and about, one another grew through their shared experience in AJC's Project Understanding, a biannual weekend retreat for thirty-two young leaders of the Black and Jewish communities. The two truly enjoy each other's company, sharing holiday dinners and celebrating life experiences together.

About Gabby

Gabby is a genuine connector who is passionate about bringing people and organizations together to accomplish big dreams. The Coral Springs, Florida, native and graduate of the University of Florida now lives in Atlanta with her husband and young son. She spends her time at the intersection of business and social good as a creator of movements around important topics like mental health, leadership, diplomacy, film, and women's empowerment.

About Candace

Candace is a technology and marketing expert working in the finance, telecomm, and healthcare industries. Always one to champion the importance of work-life balance, she enjoys adventure travel, scifi, and game nights during her free time. A native of Newport News, Virginia, Candace graduated from Clark Atlanta University and then settled in Atlanta. She enjoys volunteering in the community through organizations that focus on helping women and children in need, such as the Junior League and United Way.

Made in the USA
Columbia, SC
29 October 2024